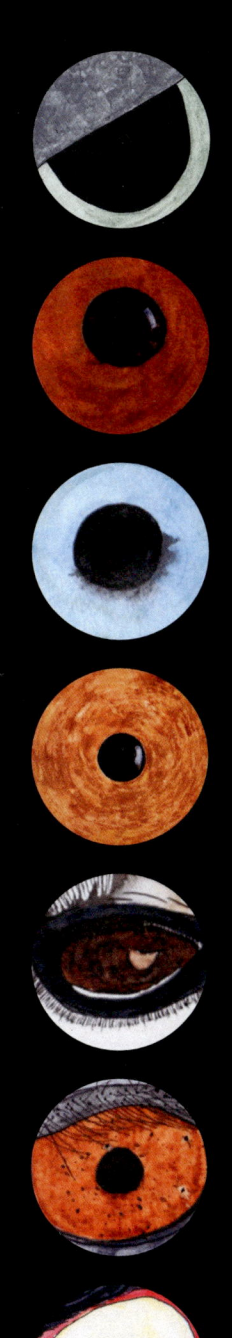

EYE SEE...
AFRICA

Author & Illustrator
Dawnanne Chase

Thanks to all of my immediate family, extended family and friends who have shown support and love with my vision and also for supporting me in all of my life endeavours. You have all helped me in some way to get to this point in my life.

A loving thank you to my parents Gene and Sandy Mignogna, they shaped me into the person I am today.

A warm thank you to Micheline Gauron, she taught me the basics of watercolor in a way that only she could. "Micki" was a character and an amazing artist. In class when I would ask her for advice on my work she would say "you know what to do, just do it" She pushed me to build my artistic talents while instilling confidence in my abilities. I am sure she is looking down from the ethers with pride.

A special thanks to Aaron "AJ" Armstrong, an energetic life coach who helped to pull this book out of me. Thank you for the encouragement and to help me to see my strengths and potential. And Marissa Armstrong for being an amazing cheerleader. And to all of the life coaches that have helped me along the way.

And to the Universe for answering me when I asked for guidance and for leading me to Catalina Castells. A fellow artist and friend that continued to show me that I can do this, while putting together this book. Your patience and artistic knowledge is priceless. You listened to my ideas and put it all together exactly the way I envisioned.

And to all that encouraged me while creating this book, adults and children alike. The enthusiasm from all of you while looking at my illustrations propelled me to keep going, thank you!

Book layout and design by Catalina Castells, see more of her work at CatalinaCastells.com.

First Edition

Published by BookBaby

I dedicate this book to my incredible sons, Tony, Colby, Zac and Dallas, their beautiful partners and all of my Grandbabies.

The time spent with all of you over the years has allowed me to revisit my childhood over and over again. I love you all so much.

This bird was around
during the times of
Ancient Egypt and
the Dinosaurs

I am part of the
Pelican Family

I have a large beak
that looks like a
wooden shoe

WHO AM EYE?

SHOEBILL

The Shoebill grows
to the size of an
average adult

They make a
noise that sounds
like a helicopter

The male and female
work together as
parents building a
nest and taking turns
sitting on their eggs

From the Cat family, known as The King of the Jungle

We live in families called Prides

Most feared predator in Africa

WHO AM EYE?

LION

Lions cannot purr but
their roar can be heard
4 to 5 miles away

Male Lions have a
majestic mane around
their neck

Males and females
work together to raise
their cubs

This animal is the tallest on earth, with the longest legs and neck

I spend most of my life standing and eating

My tongue is a dark bluish black color

WHO AM EYE?

WEST AFRICAN GIRAFFE

Giraffes are very curious animals

Giraffes only sleep 5 to 30 minutes per day, but take 1 to 2 minute naps all day long

The dark color of their tongue is a protection from sunburn because they eat 17 to 20 hours per day

I lived here among
the Dinosaurs

One of Africa's most
beautiful birds

My name comes from
the crown of feathers
on my head

WHO AM EYE?

GREY CROWNED CRANE

They spend most
of the day looking
for food in grassy
shallow waters and
ponds

When they walk they
stamp their feet
hard on the ground
to disturb insects so
they can eat them

To attract a mate
they do a crazy
dance, moving their
feet and jumping,
bowing and making a
loud honking noise

As heavy as a small car, I am the third largest mammal

I have two horns on my head

I have 3 toes on all four feet

WHO AM EYE?

NORTHERN WHITE RHINOCEROS

Rhinos aren't afraid of any animals but are afraid of humans

If their big horn breaks off it can grow back

Rhinos love to play and lay in the mud which protects their skin from the sun

This is one of the smallest
in the primate family, at
only 12 inches tall

I can jump seven times
my height

Related to the Lemurs
of Madagascar

WHO AM EYE?

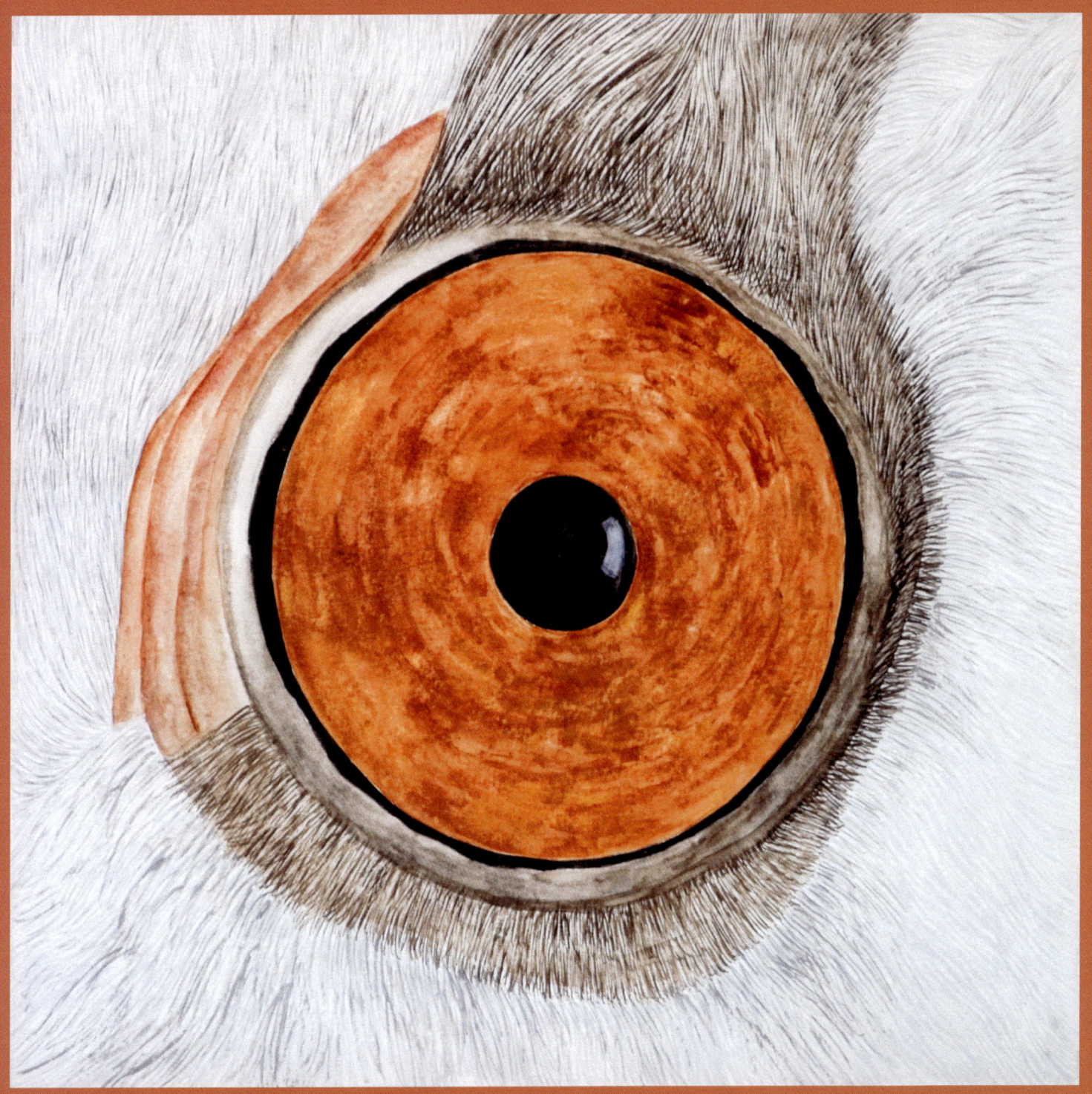

GALAGOS

The nickname of the
Galagos is Bush Baby
due to the loud crying
sounds they make much
like a baby

They have huge eyes
that cannot move to
look around without
turning their head

At the end of the night
they all yell out a special
night time call, signalling
the others that it is time
to sleep

The Largest Bird
in the world, but
cannot fly

Fastest Running two
legged animal

This bird was around
with the Dinosaurs

WHO AM EYE?

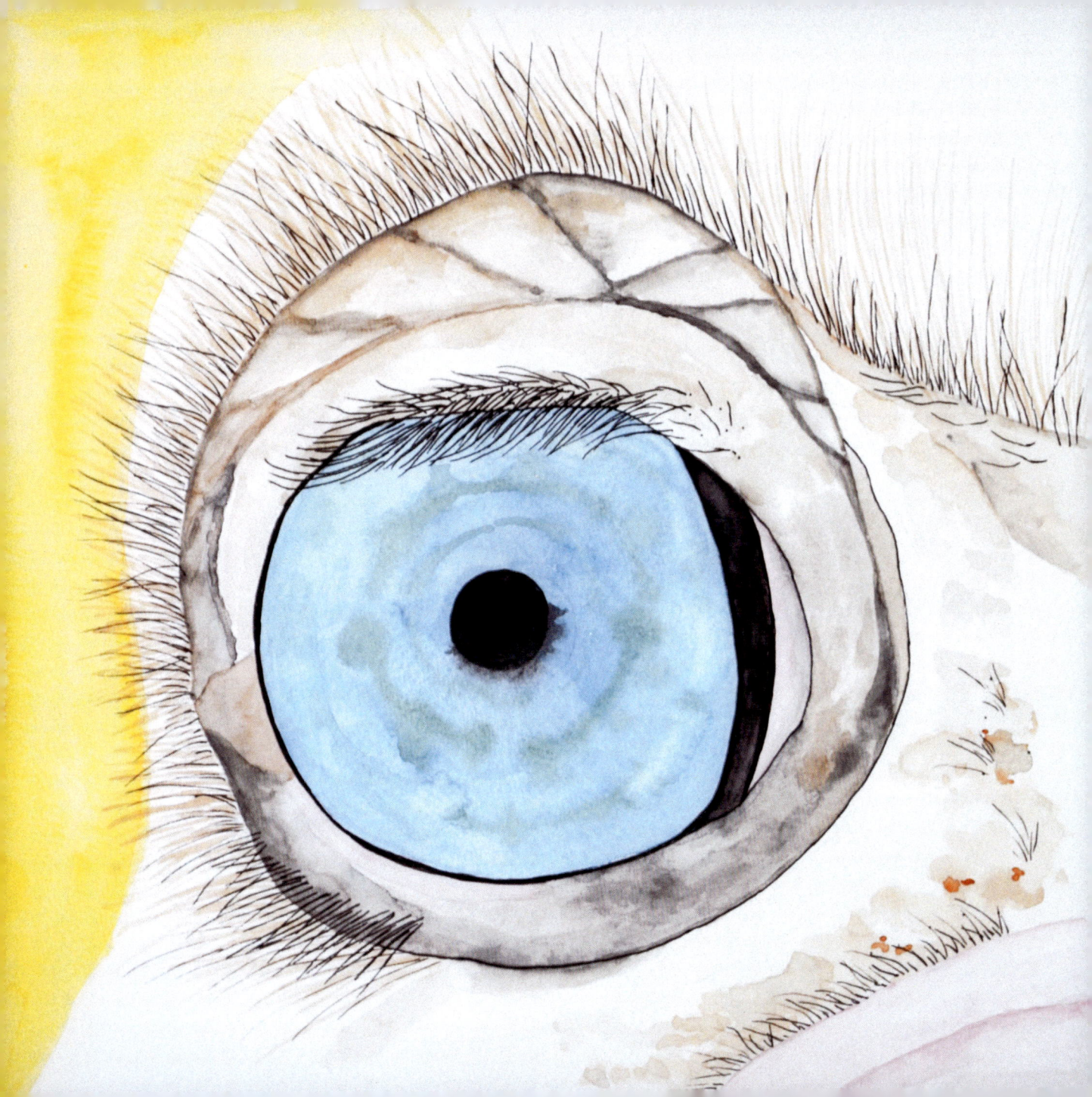

COMMON OSTRICH

Strongest Bird in
the World

Lays the largest egg
of any living bird

Has the strongest kick
that can harm people
and large animals

One of the worlds greatest
surprise attackers

Strongest Bite in the
animal kingdom

This Reptile is a
freshwater hunter

WHO AM EYE?

AFRICAN NILE CROCODILE

This animal can hold their breath under water for 10 minutes while waiting to attack.

Every tooth is hollow with a new tooth growing inside waiting to replace a lost tooth

They have 64 teeth at all times, and can have as many as 3,000 teeth in their lifetime.

This animal is from the Cat family and is the fastest running animal in the world

My name means The Spotted One, and I can have 2000 to 3000 spots on my body

When hunting and running after my prey, my tail is used to steer and balance my body

WHO AM EYE?

CHEETAH

This cat hunts for food in groups during the day to avoid fighting with other animals

Cheetahs cannot roar but they make a sound like a bird chirping

They can run so fast that sometimes their paws don't touch the ground, as if they are flying

I eat mostly bones
from dead animals
that I find

This bird is one of
the highest flying
birds in the world

I can live to the age
of 45 years old

WHO AM EYE?

BEARDED VULTURE

The eyes of this beautiful bird are red because the eye is full of blood

The name Bearded Vulture comes from the feathers on their face resembling a beard

Bearded vultures will rub soil into their feathers on their head to make them look scary to their prey

This reptilian spends
most of its time in trees

I have a very
poisonous bite

I am shy and nervous and
spend all my time alone

WHO AM EYE?

GREEN MAMBA

Sleeps all day and
hunts all night

One of the fastest and
deadliest land snakes

Only goes on the ground
to look for water and
food or to lay in the sun

The Biggest Land animal
weighing in at 13,000 to
19,000 pounds

We travel in large
groups called Herds

Because of our large
size we have no enemies
in the animal kingdom

WHO AM EYE?

AFRICAN ELEPHANT

Elephants are the
only mammal that
cannot jump

A baby elephant will suck
their trunk for comfort
just like a human baby
sucks their thumb

They show happiness
and sadness by
laughing and crying

These dogs are great
hunters and work
together to hunt for food

The nickname of this
animal from the dog
family is "Painted Wolf"

They all have different
markings on their fur

WHO AM EYE?

AFRICAN WILD DOG

They only have 4
toes on each foot

The African Wild dog
has a powerful bite

When any dog is sick
they all take care of
one another

One of the Largest
Monkeys in the world

I have a colorful
face and rump

I live in large groups
with up to 40 that
are called Troops

WHO AM EYE?

MANDRILL

When upset they will bob
their head up and down
and slap the ground

They show their colorful
rump to attract a mate

A shy monkey that
communicates with
grunts and high pitched
sounds while showing
their teeth